What Can Rabbit See?

Lucy Cousins

TAMBOURINE BOOKS

New York

This is Rabbit.
With his glasses
he can see very
well.

What can Rabbit

see in the hedge?

What can Rabbit see in the pond?

what can Rabbit see in the grass?

What can Rabbit see in the hutch?

What can Rabbit see in the sky at bedtime?

Copyright © 1991 by Lucy Cousins
First published in Great Britain by Walker Books Ltd.

Library of Congress Cataloging in Publication Data

Cousins, Lucy. What can Rabbit see? / Lucy Cousins. p. cm.
Summary: The reader is asked what Rabbit can see with his glasses
when he looks in the grass, in the sky, and other places.
[1. Eyeglasses–Fiction. 2. Rabbits–Fiction. 3. Picture
puzzles.] I. Title.
PZ7.C83175W1 1991 [E]–dc20 90-21213 CIP AC
ISBN 0-688-10454-1

Printed and bound in Hong Kong by Imago
1 3 5 7 9 10 8 6 4 2
First U.S. edition